Bag Lady

A Short Story by Liela Marie Fuller

ISBN-13: 978-0-9961289-9-5
ISBN-10: 0-9961289-9-9

Jadora's Child Publishing
Minneapolis, MN
www.ThoughtsofaThankfulHeart.com

K – Thank you for always being the inspiration I need even when you don't realize it.
#ToTheFuture

Bag Lady was a woman on a mission. Two weeks ago, while checking her mail, she received an unmarked letter giving her explicit instructions about a wonderful opportunity.

Dearest Heart,

I have been watching you and I am ready to take you to the next step. You've been asking me to usher you into better and give you more and the time has come. You've waited long enough and you've passed almost every test, but there is just one more you must pass before you can move through the doorway to wealth. If you're ready, meet me at the 29th Avenue Rail Station by door number 111 on December 2nd – that's 2 weeks from today. I hope I see you there. Pack light as only you can go through the doorway. See you soon!

While there was no address on the envelope and the letter was unsigned, she knew exactly who sent the letter – it was from God. As soon as she finished reading the letter, Bag Lady ran up to her apartment to pack her bags. She was extremely excited to move from her present into a bright and certain future. She was excited about new opportunities and new doors being opened for her. She was excited to walk through the door she prayed would open. As she packed her bags, she thought, "what perfect timing He has! My lease is up December 2nd and I still have not found a place I like! How impeccable is His timing!" As she danced around packing, she wondered what it would be like to walk through the door. She wondered what her next home would look like and what other beautiful surprises awaited her on the other side.

Two weeks seem to move so slow for Bag Lady. It was like she was living life in slow motion. One day while she was working she gazed at the clock for the time, 11am and when she looked up again it was only 11:02. She was sure that more than 2 minutes had gone by, but everything was moving at a snail's pace including time. She could not wait to see what He had for her and it felt like time was purposely moving slower than a snail. The slow pace of every day made her feel as if time were teasing her, but not even the slow pace of time could steal her joy.

When the two weeks were up, and the day finally arrived, she made her way to the bank to retrieve all the money she had because she was sure she would need it. *"I wonder if I can fit all of my stuff through this doorway. I brought everything I needed with me because I didn't want to leave anything behind. Even though He told me that He wouldn't let some stuff pass through, I brought everything I have because I need it all. I would not dream of leaving everything behind, so we'll just need to make this work somehow. My clothes, my wigs, my weaves, and all of my curling irons and flat irons are in that bag,"* she says as points to the large bag rolling behind her.

There were at least 20 bags surrounding bag lady and she believed that each bag's contents were necessary for her life. As she continued to recount what she packed, she wondered *"I am sure He wasn't talking about my shoes when he said to leave everything you own and follow me. He must know that I cannot be seen without them. I mean what respectable woman goes anywhere without 2 pairs of flats, 4 pairs of heels, booties, and knee length boots. Surely, He did not mean my shoes!"*

Bag Lady did not know exactly where she was going, but when He sent her an invitation to her next, she could not refuse. As she read the invitation again she noticed the caveat He placed on it warning her there was only room for her and her things would need to stay behind, but she refused to believe He meant those words. She knew that as soon as He saw her and how amazing her things were, He would take back what He said and allow her to keep her things.

She arrived at the station and at the door he specified, but she noticed that she was the only one standing there – her and all her baggage. *"This doorway sure is narrow, but I've gotta get through it,"* she said. She knew that on the other side of that door was her purpose, her destiny, her marriage and her ministry, but she just needed to get through it – her and all of her stuff.

As she stood there contemplating how to get through the door with all her things, she saw a woman off to the side with no shoes and she thought maybe I should give her mine. As much as she didn't want to lose her place in line, she felt led to give this woman some shoes. She walked over lugging all of her baggage to the woman lying on the ground with very little and Bag Lady said, "*I noticed your feet were bare and, in that bag, right there I've got some shoes. Open it and take what you need.*"

The woman with no shoes exclaimed, "*I just prayed for some shoes and here you are with more than enough to offer me just what I need! Thank you, Jesus!*" The Woman with No Shoes tried on several pairs of the shoes in Bag Lady's bag to see which one fit her right and miraculously they all seemed to fit her just right. Bag Lady could not understand how they all fit the woman so well and she further could not understand the words she heard come out of her mouth, "*Take them all, I can get more.*" Bag Lady thought someone else was talking in her place because there was no way she would give up all her shoes to some random, albeit precious, lady at the station. The Woman with No Shoes called over some of her friends and she shared the shoes she received from Bag Lady because there were so many others around her without, she could not dream of hoarding them all to herself.

Bag Lady turned and walked away, in shock over what just happen, but feeling a little lighter. As she made her way back to the doorway, she noticed a woman walking out of a pizza place with clothes that didn't match the season. Bag Lady thought, *"Clearly this woman knows it is winter outside, but why is she dressed for summer?"* Bag Lady stopped the woman and asked her for her name. The woman said she was Wealth Gone Wrong, and she had lost all her riches because she made all the wrong decisions. Bag Lady was intrigued with

Wealth Gone Wrong's story and as Bag Lady stood there waiting to hear her story, she wondered how Wealth could have gone so wrong.

It was a sad story really, Wealth had come to her and she had not taken the time to get her mind and heart lined up for where it would take her. Instead, she kept the same mindset and the same things so when she moved into her wealthy place, her mindset followed her along with her ghetto and poverty mentalities. When the windows would break in her home, she would duct tape cardboard or newspaper up, because she didn't know whom to call. No one had ever told Wealth Gone Wrong where to go or who to call to fix things in the wealthy place, so she got it all wrong. She had loud parties with all her family and friends and since she didn't teach them how to act or treat her in her wealthy place, they continued to treat her as they did before wealth came and that brought law enforcement to her door with noise complaints and neighborhood violations.

"*I thought I had it all together! I had pulled myself up by my bootstraps, but I forgot to leave the childish things behind and I trusted everyone with a story to tell. I gave all my money away to causes I thought were worthy and I never consulted the One who gave me the seed to begin with. I think if I had, He would have told me that the seed was too precious for that infertile ground. I let my thoughts and my emotions guide me and my seed ended up dying – no revival and no funeral – just hijacked, hindered, and stolen. Soon, I lost everything I owned and there was nothing left. I finally decided to listen to the*

One and He told me to come here to get a slice of pizza. I didn't think it was Him because this was the last $3.00 I had and there was so much more I needed, but I figured He wanted me to eat so here I am. What's your story?"

Bag Lady was shocked and but she said, *"I'm on my way to a new place and in that bag, I've got some clothes, curling irons, flat irons, weaves, wigs, and more. You are more than welcome to it, in fact, it's all yours."* Wealth Gone Wrong cheered, *"THANK YOU LORD!"* For she had just wondered how she would make it through the winter with nothing more than the summer shorts and tee on her back but now she could begin again with a new wardrobe and even a new business – Wealth Transfer Wigs. Wealth decided that she would start small and work her way up, listening to the One who'd brought her here for what she thought was just a slice of pizza. Wealth Gone Wrong was so excited she jumped up, hugged Bag Lady, and kissed her on the cheek. Bag Lady could not believe she had once again given away another bag of her precious things. While there was a need, she did not think she should be the one to give her stuff away, but the only recourse was the thought she could recoup it all in her next.

As Bag Lady walked away, she felt led to turn back to Wealth Gone Wrong and do something even crazier. She heard "give her the money you've been hiding in bag #3." Bag Lady was angry now; the money in bag #3 was her seed money - $120,000 of seed money. She had worked hard for that money and while she had more money, this was for a specific purpose and clearly not for some lady who had squandered her money away because she didn't listen. *"NO!"* Bag Lady exclaimed, *"I'm not doing that, YOU ARE CRAZY if you think I'm giving that woman, who just told me that she lost everything because she didn't listen, my hard-earned money. You are crazy!"* Bag Lady was angry, but she heard His voice again, but this time there was more. *"Are you a good listener all the time? Did I not just give you a command to do something, yet you sit here arguing with me. Tell me when was the last time you knew the beginning and the end? When was the last time you knew what the end of the world would look like or even the end of your story, let alone hers? GIVE HER THE MONEY YOU'VE BEEN HIDING IN BAG #3."* And as quickly as the voice came, it left, and Bag

Lady felt such conviction she reached around and grabbed bag #3 and with a hung head, handed it to Wealth Gone Wrong. When Wealth Gone Wrong opened the bag, she nearly fainted. She had to sit down so she didn't fall on the ground.

Wealth Gone Wrong wept, looked at Bag Lady and said, "*Why are you giving me this; you don't know me?*" Bag Lady said, "*Because He said, that's why, Because He said.*" Wealth Gone Wrong was floored and without words. She could not move because her legs were like jelly and her mind was going a mile a minute. Bag Lady said, "*God Bless you! Walk back into your wealthy place.*" Bag Lady could not believe the words that were coming out of her mouth. She could not believe it. As she walked back to the doorway, her load felt lighter and she wondered if she could now go through the narrow doorway.

Bag Lady could see the door from where she was standing and there was no one waiting in line but also no one there to greet her so she figured it must not be time. She took a seat and decided that she'd have a cup of tea. As she sat there, she looked at her bags and three were missing, but when she thought of where they had gone, she was happy to be part of the process even though it didn't feel good in the moment. As she looked at her remaining bags - Pride, Self-Centeredness, Selfishness, Past Wrongs, Hurt, Grudges, Animosity, Doubt, and Fear - she wondered what He would do with them. She knew these were not bags she could give to anyone else and she knew they would be a hindrance to her, but she had to bring them with her because they were part of her. She also looked at bags #1, 2, 4 & 5 and remembered the treasure she had stored up in them and she smiled because she was still a wealthy woman. As she sipped her tea and closed her eyes to reflect on what awaited her on the other side of the doorway, she felt pain and burning in her arms. She could not figure it out. She tried opening her eyes, but it was like they were glued shut and all she could do was call out for help.

"Ouch! Stop it! You're hurting me. Someone please Help me," she cried, but no one came to help her. There was no one there but her – alone sitting at a table surrounded by all her baggage. The more she fought, the more it hurt and the more it hurt the more she fought. After what seemed like an eternity, she opened her eyes again and she

immediately noticed that bags were missing. "*I've been robbed*," she screamed. "*Someone help me!*" But no one came and when she looked around, she was back at the narrow doorway, alone again. The station was empty – there was no one there but her, her baggage, and the narrow doorway. As she looked down at her baggage, she realized there were just 4 bags left – Pride, Self-Centeredness, Selfishness, Past Wrongs, Hurt, Grudges, Animosity, Doubt and Fear were taken from her. "*Where did these bags go? Who took my stuff? How can I go walk into the narrow doorway so empty?*" She remembered the 4 bags she had left, and she said, "*This will have to do.*"

She went closer to the door way and it seemed to get smaller – like it fit her body completely but if that was the case there was no way she would get her 4 bags of money through with her. What was she going to do?

As she stood there contemplating, 2 men came by – one she knew and one she didn't. The man who knew her practically raised her and taught her all she knew about the One. She spoke to them both but only the stranger spoke back. She called the man she knew by his name, *"Uncle Charlie! It's me, don't you see me?"* Uncle Charlie looked right at her glanced through the door waiting for her and ignored her. She could not believe it, nor could she understand what was happening so she stood there crying. The stranger said, *"You don't know what's happening, do you?"* Bag Lady shook her head no and sobbed. *"You, precious one, are so close to your destiny that it is making you glow. You are so close to stepping into your purpose that it is as if a beam of light is coming out of every pore of your body. While you may not see it, those who know you and even some who don't see it and some are happy but some are not. You are about to walk into a great destiny beyond this narrow doorway and if I just look at you and look into the doorway, I can see the spectacularly amazing thing God is doing and I applaud you for sticking it out, but others see it and are jealous because they missed their opportunity through disobedience or sin. You are right there; you've just got one more thing to do before you can walk into that narrow doorway."*

Bag Lady was astounded by the stranger's words and she was about to say she didn't know what to do and then she heard

Him. *"Give the stranger the money in bags 1, 2, 4, and 5. What I have for you on the other side is much more."* By now, Bag Lady understood that she needed to heed His voice, so she reached down and handed the stranger the bags. As the stranger opened them, one at a time, he smiled and changed. Bag Lady said, *"That's never happened before"* and she said to him, *"you're changing,"* and he smiled and said, *"I know."* Bag Lady wondered if she had heard Him right, and she thought, *"Maybe this wasn't good ground. Oh no, I don't want to end up like Wealth Gone Wrong. I need this to be good ground."*

As the stranger opened the last bag, his transformation was complete, and she saw Him. She saw Jesus! She knelt at his feet and worshipped Him. *"Why did you disguise yourself to me?"* He said, *"Because I needed you to give to someone you thought wasn't me and you did. You served the stranger just as you would have served me not knowing it was me and you have been rewarded,"* He said as he pointed to the narrow doorway. She could now see all that she had not seen before, red carpet going up to the door and a limo waiting on the other side. Where it was once a dark doorway, there was now a marvelous light.

Jesus said to her, *"the way has been made and while I cannot promise you won't have trials know that I am always with you wherever you go."* She smiled and walked into the narrow doorway that fit her just right and on the other side she found destiny, fame, fortune and love – all the things He promised her. After she crossed the threshold, she barely remembered the shoes, clothes, wigs, weaves and money she had given up. She didn't recall the Pride, Self-Centeredness, Selfishness, Past Wrongs, Hurt, Grudges, Animosity, Doubt and Fear snatched from her. All she knew was the peace here in the place beyond the narrow doorway – the place without fear.

And as for the Woman with No Shoes and Wealth Gone Wrong, they each had their narrow doorways as well and as they helped Bag Lady get through hers, she unknowingly helped them get through theirs.

The moral of the story is this, sometimes God wants to remove the very things we are trying to hold onto and when we release it (or He takes it from us) we can make it to the place He's calling us to. Along the way, we are assigned to help others make it through their door too but we can never get caught up on where they are or who they are because everyone has a story. Everyone has a reason they are where they are; our job isn't to judge but to help them make it through to their destiny. So, Bag Lady, what's your story?

About the Author

Liela Marie Fuller is an Author, Entrepreneur, Journal Creator and Prayer Warrior. Liela is the owner of Jadora's Child Publishing and Heavenly Help Computer Solutions. Liela is also the founder of the Minnesota Prayer Hotline – a 24-hour prayer hotline for those in the Twin Cities and beyond.

Liela enjoys praying, writing, reading and spending time at any of the 10,000 lakes in her adopted home state of Minnesota.

You can connect with Liela on Facebook, Twitter, Instagram and on her website www.ThoughtsofaThankfulHeart.com

www.ingramcontent.com/pod-product-compliance
Lightning Source LLC
Chambersburg PA
CBHW031905170626
46807CB00004B/1907